This Walker book belongs to:

For Mara with all our love

S.H & H.C

First published 1995 by Walker Books Ltd
87 Vauxhall Walk, London SE11 5HJ

This edition published 2003

4 6 8 10 9 7 5

This book has been typeset in Garamond

Printed in China

British Library Cataloguing in Publication Data: a catalogue record for this book is available from the British Library.

ISBN-13: 978-0-7445-9812-4
ISBN-10: 0-7445-9812-5

www.walkerbooks.co.uk

This is the BEAR and the Bad Little Girl

Sarah Hayes illustrated by **Helen Craig**

WALKER BOOKS
AND SUBSIDIARIES
LONDON • BOSTON • SYDNEY • AUCKLAND

This is the bear
who went out to eat.

This is the dog
who stayed in the street.

This is the girl
with the curly hair

who said she really
liked the bear.

This is the dog
who put out a paw

and tripped the woman
who came in the door …

... which pushed the people

waiting to pay …

… and made the waiter
drop the tray.

Mamma mia!
My marshmallow pie!

This is the boy
all covered in cream

who went to the kitchen
to wash his face clean.

This is the girl
with the curly hair

who said, "You're coming with me, bear."

This is the girl who
walked down the street

holding the bear
by one of his feet.

This is the dog
who thought it was fun

when the bad little girl
began to run.

This is the girl
who ran faster and faster

but this is the dog
who ran right past her.

This is the girl
who gave the bear back
and said he was
only a baggy old sack.

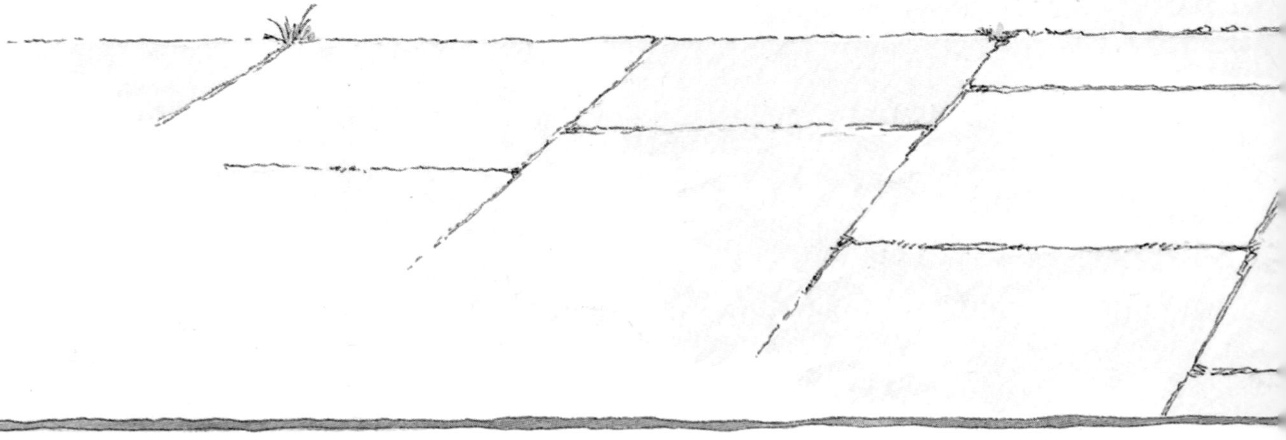

Fred!
I'm not a sack!
I didn't want him anyway.

This is the boy
who said, “I don’t care
if he’s saggy or baggy,
he’s still *my* bear.”

So there!

All four *This is the Bear* stories

Sarah Hayes is the author of many books for children, including the *This is the Bear* quartet; *Mary, Mary*; *Happy Christmas*; and *Eat Up, Gemma* (shortlisted for the Smarties Book Prize).

Helen Craig is a widely acclaimed illustrator of books for children, whose work includes *The Town Mouse and the Country Mouse* (shortlisted for the Smarties Book Prize); *Rosie's Visitors*; and the hugely popular stories about *Angelina Ballerina*, who has featured in her own animated TV series.

www.walker.co.uk